ALIEN ATTRACTION

A TAUREAN WARRIORS PREQUEL

MELODY BECKETT

Alien Attraction: A Taurean Warriors Prequel by Melody Beckett
Published by Bronzewing Books

Copyright © 2022 Melody Beckett

www.melodybeckett.com

For permissions contact: hello@melodybeckett.com

Cover by Kasmit Covers

Editing by Valerie Gray of Edit A Book

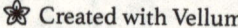 Created with Vellum

For those who never thought their dreams would come true.

CONTENT WARNING

This books contains:

- Explicit language
- Battle scenes
- Death (on page)
- Large insectoid aliens

This title was previously published as "Freeing Her Alien Warrior"

ALIEN ATTRACTION

CHAPTER ONE

Oren

Oren Ka'Ress cursed as the controls of the small spaceship strained under his hands. He was nowhere near the location where he was meant to rendezvous with the large intergalactic starship he called home. The Starship Zataras was a small city of close to five thousand Taureans. It was designed for combat and housed warriors and support crew who, like Oren, fought in the escalating war with the Xakul. The ship shook and rattled, and Oren cursed again. That solar storm yesterday had definitely fried something, and he had no way to fix it until he made it safely back to the Zataras.

A flashing light in a panel above his head caught his attention. Thank the gods! He reached up and pushed the control; the display flickered to show a blue and green planet slowly rotating into view. His long-range sensors were still working, and it looked like he had a trip to Earth in his immediate future. He had never been there before,

1

but at least it was nearby and he could land and wait to be picked up.

An engineer he was not. Sure, he knew how to do minor repairs, and the ship's artificial intelligence was pretty good at self-diagnosis, but this problem was beyond his capabilities. The AI had stopped responding hours ago, and Oren had resorted to using manual controls. He no longer trusted the navigation system not to blast him into a star.

Being an intelligence officer had its benefits. It was a change from the usual military duties and, although he worked alone most of the time, he didn't mind it, but this job had him slightly worried. Right now he had two concerns: getting this dinky little spaceship fixed, and handing over his dangerous cargo as quickly as possible.

Turning the shuttle towards Earth, he engaged the cloaking device which would shield the small ship from observation by the planet's inhabitants, not sure if it would even respond. The solar storm had damaged the navigation system and the AI, so it surprised him when the cloak actually started working. It made no sense, but right now he was happy to have one less thing to worry about.

Shaking his head, he watched as the planet grew larger on the screen, finally filling it. There was no shuttle traffic to or from the surface. Curious. He swiped across a tablet, and he knew immediately there were no longer-distance orbiting transit hubs either. Just great. There was no way they had FTL, or Faster Than Light capabilities, so there was no way his shuttle could be repaired here.

He sighed, "Shit. What else can go wrong?"

An ear-splitting electronic wail filled the cabin, and Oren winced at the sound.

"That was a hypothetical question!" He said to himself.

With some difficulty he reached for his harness and strapped himself in to the pilot's seat, still not able to let go of the controls. The shuttle lurched and began accelerating rapidly towards the surface of the planet.

"Fuck. Fuck. Fuck!"

Teeth bared in a snarl, he fought to control the shuttle's descent towards the planet. The cloud shifted and a great expanse of water appeared, filling the entire screen. "No way! I am not fucking drowning today!"

Oren flicked rapidly through the information on the tablet and selected the first available spot of land that appeared to be, at least superficially, uninhabited. With a bit of luck, he could land and make some basic repairs to get the AI up and running again. Then he could at least continue on his journey. But right now this spaceship was going nowhere except down.

The shuttle shook and shuddered as it entered the atmosphere, and Oren fought to control the descent. The wailing noise in the cabin became an incessant drone, and he thumped his massive fist against the controls, grunting in satisfaction when the noise stopped.

The ocean rushed towards him, and in the distance, land was visible. As the shuttle finally decelerated, and Oren could adjust the flight path towards a distant desert bordered by mountains. The flat land would make the landing a little easier.

Looking out the window, Oren could see the land and sea racing towards him. He adjusted the shuttle's trajectory enough to aim towards the land, and within a minute he had cleared the mountains and land stretched beneath him.

But the shuttle was moving too fast.

Oren checked the scans again and found an empty stretch of land in the distance, and fought to slow the shuttle. This would not be a "soft" landing. For the first time in a long time, he prayed, asking to make it home in one piece.

It was early evening, and the land was swathed in darkness. This part of the planet did not face the sun, which he was thankful for. Maybe one thing could go right this day.

The ground loomed below; the shuttle slowed but not enough, and rather than a gentle, controlled descent, it hit the ground hard with a loud crump. Lockers opened, spilling their contents into the small space, as the shuttle jerked and bounced against the uneven ground, finally sliding along until it hit a monstrous boulder and flipped upside down with a bang and a cloud of smoke.

Strapped into his seat, Oren covered his head protectively, waiting for the shuttle to settle as it listed one way, then the other.

Great. He was upside down.

He lifted his wrist and tapped the screen on his comm. The device on his wrist acted as a multi-purpose communicator, timepiece, health monitor... basically it did everything. But it wasn't working.

He tapped the screen again. Nothing.

"Computer, what's the status of our on board guest?"

Oren asked as blood rushed to his head from being upside down. He had to get out of this seat.

"The Xakul captive is unconscious and secured in the holding cell."

That was a relief. The bastard had been hard enough to secure in that cell in the first place. It took five of them to do it. Working as an intelligence operative in the Taurean military, Oren now knew more about this vicious species than he had ever imagined, and he would be glad to hand him over. They had captured this one on a nearby planet, Mars, he thought the humans called it, after most of its fellow soldiers had been chased off by the Taureans. Oren had been transporting it to the Zataras to be taken to his home planet, Taurus, for interrogation and... well, he really didn't want to know what else Taurean Intelligence had planned.

One worry out of the way, he turned his attention to the clip on his harness. It could not be undone with his weight pulling on it, so he lifted his foot and pulled out the small knife he kept in his boot. Holding the harness in one hand, he used the other to quickly slice through the webbing, which gave way suddenly, dropping Oren's large frame onto the ceiling of the ship, hitting something hard and sharp.

"Oof," his breath left him in a rush and he felt something crack in his chest. Pain flooded through him. He held still for a second, trying to breathe through it. He shifted tentatively, pain spearing his side when he tried to move.

A rib. It had to be a rib.

Oren looked around the cabin, trying to orient himself. The area was a mess, but right now he needed some first aid equipment. The medical gear was stored in a locker that should be... aha! There it was!

He stood slowly, bracing himself against the walls as he carefully stepped over the fallen detritus. The door on the medical locker was bashed in. Fuck it. He grabbed the handle and yanked on it, tearing the door from its hinges and causing himself additional pain.

What was one more broken thing in a shuttle that was probably beyond its best before date?

He fished around inside the cabinet, his fingers brushing up against the container that contained the medi-scanner. The handheld device fit in the palm of his hand and could diagnose and heal a range of common illnesses and internal injuries. Oren sighed in relief as he retrieved it.

He flicked the button on the side, and the small, oblong device beeped sadly.

"Shit." It was out of charge, and now completely useless. Oren tossed it aside and ran a hand over his closely shorn hair.

Both the medical scanner and his comm were out of battery power. He had checked them as part of his pre-mission equipment protocol, and that was only a few days ago. They both should have weeks of charge left. The solar storm must have affected the batteries somehow.

What now? He needed to heal, and he was no medic. He groaned, then winced and clutched his side. Right now he needed to get the hell out of this shuttle.

"Computer, is the atmosphere of this planet breathable?" He probably should have checked earlier, but beggars couldn't be choosers.

"*Earth has an atmosphere composed of 78.1% Nitrogen, 20.9% Oxygen—*"

"Yeah, yeah, thanks for the chemistry lesson, but is it breathable?"

"*Yes, Earth's atmosphere is breathable for Taureans.*"

The ship's main hatch was jammed shut, and there was no way to move it, so the emergency escape was the only option. Feeling relieved that at least he wouldn't suffocate, Oren pulled the handle and a second later it released. A loud hissing noise filled the small space and Oren felt the floor... ceiling... tilt as the pressure changed. He dragged himself up through the hatch and dropped onto the rocky ground outside. The twelve-foot landing was rough, causing him to pass out in pain. But just before he jumped, he saw a pair of lights moving towards him.

CHAPTER TWO

Amelia

It was dark when Dr. Amelia O'Malley pulled up to the boom gate at the main entrance to the military base where she worked. The chilly night breeze whipped her hair around her face as she wound down the window of her Jeep to swipe her pass against the scanner pad. Scrubs certainly didn't provide the best protection in the cool night air. As hot as it was during the day in the Nevada desert, the temperatures plummeted at night.

The guard in the booth lifted a hand to wave her inside as the green light flashed and the boom gate lifted. Amelia raised a hand in return, winding up the window and turning to look out the windshield at the long, dark road that led into the base. A series of sparsely spaced streetlights lit the long, empty road that disappeared into the darkness.

Amelia put the Jeep into drive, and a few minutes later, after bumping along the gravel road, she turned toward a cluster of buildings that were located around the base hospital. She pulled into her usual parking spot and, turning off the engine, let out an enormous sigh. She was about to begin another shift, in a long line of shifts, over days that blurred into one another. But, thankfully, not for much longer.

Amelia had joined Earth's newly formed Space Force after graduating from medical school, thinking it was her best chance to make a difference. She had bought into the marketing, the promise of humanity finally exploring space, and making a new start away from the planet that they had almost systematically and comprehensively destroyed.

But not long after joining Space Force, she quickly realized her mistake.

With only a few months left of her contract, she was getting out. She had never even seen the inside of a shuttle, let alone made it into space. She hadn't been included in the terraforming project on Mars, which was the shining beacon of hope for the future of humanity. The irony of starting anew was not lost on Amelia.

She wanted to do more than sit on a dying planet and watch the world crumble. She wanted to make a difference and, naively, thought that Space Force would be her opportunity. Scoffing at herself, she opened the door to the Jeep and stepped into the frosty night.

The latest in a long line of disappointments, Amelia had been sent to Nevada, to this secret base, a few weeks earlier. She still did not know what they used the base for. That kind of information was levels of security clearance above her, and she had convinced herself that she didn't care anyway. Instead, she put her head down and just did what she was told. And, being the newest doctor on site, she always seemed to catch these late-night weekend shifts. But really, she didn't have any reason to complain. It wasn't like she had a life outside of work anyway, even if she lived in the supposed party city of Las Vegas.

Locking the Jeep behind her, Amelia climbed the short flight of stairs to the main entrance and pushed through the double doors into the main building. After making her way through a series of security checkpoints and scanner pads, she was just placing her gear inside her locker when she heard the annoyingly nasal voice of her least favorite nurse.

"Hey, Dr. Millie!"

Amelia cringed. No matter how many times she had asked Janet to not shorten her name, she still did it. Only her grandmother had ever called her Millie, and she was long gone.

Pushing the thought aside, she forced a small smile. "Hi, Janet. What's up?"

The nurse rushed towards her, leaning in conspiratorially, although they were the only people in the locker room.

"Did you hear?" Janet asked in a stage whisper, eyes wide.

"Hear what?"

"They've shut down the whole of ward five for *one* patient. And guards with huge guns are maintaining security!"

Amelia struggled not to roll her eyes. This *was* a

military base, for God's sake. A *Space Force* military base. Of course, there were guards with guns.

"I'm sure it's not—"

"And they have assigned you to his medical team!" Janet's eyes filled with sympathy. "Will you be ok?" she asked again in the same mock whisper.

Amelia shut her locker door with a bang and engaged the lock. "I'm sure I will be fine. No need to worry." She forced a smile and turned away from her colleague, pushing open the doors leading to the wards. There was no point worrying about something she couldn't change. It wasn't Janet's fault that Amelia found her so annoying. She was an excellent nurse—it was just that she made everything so dramatic.

"Alright, have a good shift!" The cheery voice of the nurse followed Amelia into the hallway. Amelia nodded to other staff members as she passed them on her way to ward five, her shoes squeaking on the vinyl floor, the familiar smell of disinfectant filling her nose. Even though she was looking forward to leaving, this place was familiar and safe. Hospitals freaked out many people but, for Amelia, they made her feel comfortable and at home. Everything was in her control in a hospital. She was in charge.

The elevator she took to up to ward five seemed to take forever. In contrast to the impressive public image of Space Force, this building was definitely old school. There didn't seem to be a budget to refurbish old facilities like this, and this elevator was a perfect example. It finally ground to a halt with an alarming screech that Amelia had long since learned to ignore.

The elevator doors opened, and she made her way

along the corridor to the double doors leading to the ward. Her ward. A ward with one patient, if what Janet said was true.

Amelia swiped her pass against the scanner pad, and the ward doors opened for her. The guard inside did have an enormous gun and, for a moment, Amelia froze. Maybe Janet had been right. What reason could there be to have someone so heavily armed in here, of all places?

The normally busy nurses' station in the center of the ward was conspicuously quiet. Amelia's brow furrowed as she turned back to the guard to ask where everyone was.

Before she could utter a word, she heard a loud noise, like a growl, coming from a room further down the hall. The sound was unlike anything she had heard before. Nevertheless, she hurried towards the room and then paused in the doorway to reconcile her brain with what she was seeing.

The largest man she had ever seen was thrashing on the bed. His feet hung over the end, his legs and wrists restrained with straps. Two of the hospital's biggest orderlies were holding the bed, trying to stop it from toppling over, while another held the patient's shoulders down.

"Quick! Give me the needle!"

Amelia's gaze shot to a doctor she had never seen before. She hadn't been at this hospital for long, but she knew all the doctors on staff. But this guy? She had never seen him before in her life. What the hell he was doing on her ward?

He was wearing military fatigues, and not scrubs like the hospital staff. He had a stethoscope around his neck and the Red Cross on the sleeve of his uniform showed he was a military doctor. She gasped as he savagely jabbed a needle into the patient's neck and then jumped back to safety.

The patient's movements slowed, his head turning towards Amelia to pierce her with the most intense blue eyes she had ever seen. Amelia felt a jolt as his eyes met hers and held her gaze, pleading with her to help him. She took an involuntary step towards the bed, but a guard reached out to stop her.

He was trying to move again, calling out in a language she did not understand. Then his movements stilled completely, and his eyes shut, and the room became completely quiet.

She released her breath in a rush, not realizing she had been holding it. The guard let her go.

"What was that language? Russian?" She asked as she approached the bed, her eyes still on the enormous man lying supine in front of her.

The military doctor answered her, "No, that was not Russian."

"Who are you?" Amelia asked.

The doctor gathered his things together, ignoring her question. "You will need to monitor the... patient... and when he wakes, you must sedate him immediately. If he gives you any trouble, contact me." He handed Amelia a plain white business card with only a phone number on it. "I will expect updates every few hours."

Amelia looked up from the card, her gaze narrowing on the doctor as he shouldered a messenger bag and attempted to brush past her. She stepped in front of him, crossing her arms and looking him square in the face, causing him to stop in his tracks.

"Who. Are. You?" she repeated her question.

"I'm with S.E.T.L. I'm the head of the medical team."

"What else can you tell me?" Amelia asked. "This is my ward. You can't just barge in and clear out all my patients! What happened to showing some professional courtesy? Do you have a name? And what does Search for Extra-Terrestrial Life want with him?" Amelia gestured towards the patient lying unmoving on the bed.

"I'm Major Sculder, but the rest of that information is classified. I'm sure you will figure it out for yourself." He smirked at her, saying he would be in touch, and then he turned to leave the room, escorted by the guards.

What a jerk, Amelia thought to herself. She looked again at the patient on the bed. She had never seen someone so large. He must be at least seven feet tall. Other than his unusual height, he looked like everyone else. She watched as his intense blue eyes finally rolled back in his head, and he relaxed into unconsciousness.

Well, this was an usual start to her shift. Things were about to get interesting.

CHAPTER THREE

Oren

The light filtering through the window hurt his eyes, and Oren hadn't even opened them yet. He groaned and rolled his head on the pillow, grimacing and turning away from the light. He tried to lift his arm to shield his eyes, but he couldn't move.

Oren's eyes flew open, and he cursed as his head pounded in pain. His heartbeat escalated, and he forced himself to breathe deeply, but breathing was painful. He had definitely damaged some ribs, but that was the least of his worries. Only years of training kept the panic at bay. He lay back, closed his eyes, and tried to calm his breathing. Moments later, he noticed someone else in the room.

"Hello, I'm Dr. O'Malley. Your ribs are badly bruised, and some may be broken, so you're bound to be in a bit of pain." The soft voice was calming, and his eyes struggled to focus on the woman as she approached the bed. She smiled and hesitantly placed a hand on his shoulder. He stilled at her touch and found himself mesmerized by her blue eyes. Eyes that were flecked with green, and crinkled in the corners when she smiled.

Where was he? He remembered the solar storm and the AI system not responding. He also remembered making a shitty landing. The next thing he knew he was being transported here by a bunch of soldiers. There was no way now he would meet Starship Zataras, as planned. He had sent out one last emergency message before he crash landed. Had they received his message? There was no way to know. One thing he knew, and that was he needed to get out of here. Someway, somehow he had to contact Starship Zataras.

The woman's soft voice drew his attention.

"You're awake sooner than I thought you would be. You must burn through the drugs quicker than we can pump them into you," she broke his gaze to fuss with the equipment. Her shapeless scrubs pulled across her hips as she bent to adjust the bed. A mass of curly red hair spilled over her shoulders and fell in front of her face.

With a huff, she straightened up and grabbed the hair in one hand and twisted it into submission on top of her head. Oren's eyes dropped to where her tunic top pulled tight against her chest, and he swallowed, his mouth suddenly dry. He had never been this close to a human before.

"What?" Her movements stilled and her brows furrowed.

He coughed, trying to clear his throat and make his intentions known by gesturing to his mouth.

"Oh, sure. You want a glass of water?" She smiled and

turned to a small table nearby to pick up a cup with a straw. She turned back and offered it to him, his head lifting from the pillow to suck the liquid through the straw, his eyes not leaving hers.

A flush moved across her cheeks, spilling down her throat, and she broke eye contact to pull away.

"Where am I?" he asked, knowing she wouldn't be able to understand him.

She turned back to him, confusion drawing her eyebrows together. "I don't understand what you're saying."

Shit. He looked at his wrist, already aware that his multi-purpose communicator, or comm, was gone, but he needed to see for himself. His comm was his lifeline when he was on missions. It was a timepiece, a universal language translator, and, most importantly, it connected him to his ship's AI, and to the battleship's communications operators. Without it, he could not fully communicate with the people on this planet. Without his comm, he was screwed.

He felt naked without it. At least his translation implant had been downloaded with the local languages before he crashed. The shortcoming of the translation implant was that it didn't translate what he spoke or read, only what he heard. It translated auditory input into Taurean, and it was highly adaptive, allowing Oren to understand what his captors were saying. However, they could not understand him.

Oren cursed, banging his head against the pillow in frustration.

"Hey, take it easy!" The woman's hand came down on his shoulder, and he stilled, turning towards her.

"You need to calm down or they'll sedate you again," she said as she tried to use gestures to show what she meant, unaware that he could understand what she was saying. She glanced over her shoulder at the door and then dropped her voice to little more than a whisper. "Well, more than we already have."

He followed her gaze to the door and spied the guard standing ready, a rifle in his hands that was unfamiliar to Oren, but it was large and it looked dangerous.

He took a deep breath to calm himself, turning his head back towards her. If he had to guess, he would say that she did not want to harm him. Even so, he felt extremely vulnerable being strapped to this bed. His wrists and ankles hurt where the restraints had bitten into his skin. He shifted slightly. He needed his comm if he was going to get out of here. And even then, he couldn't do it on his own. He needed an ally.

Oren scrutinized the woman in front of him. Her blue eyes were concerned, willing him to understand and be calm. He was going to need her to work with him. He needed to communicate with someone, and she seemed like the safest bet.

A noise in the hallway drew her attention, and she stepped away from his bed, her posture stiffening.

The door to the room opened, and a man entered wearing the same type of clothing as Amelia. Her posture had relaxed slightly, but she still appeared wary as she addressed the newcomer.

"Good morning, James. Ready to hand over?"

He approached the bed and, ignoring Oren, turned to the woman and smiled. "Sure. He was a little... unsettled when he came in with Major Sculder. How is he this morning?"

"He seems fine. Very quiet," she said as she avoided looking at Oren, her posture still tense despite her casual tone.

Oren let their conversation wash over him as he rapidly considered and discarded ideas for escape. His spaceship had likely been destroyed beyond repair, at least beyond Oren's skills, so that was not an option. If his distress signal had not been received by Starship Zataras, he might be stranded on this planet for a while. Either way, he wasn't going anywhere without his comm. He tuned back into their conversation.

"No." Amelia was protesting something that had been said, her arms now crossed over her chest.

"No?" The man laughed, crossing his arms across his chest. "You have no idea what you're messing with."

"I don't care, James. This is my patient, and he is not well enough to be moved."

The man glanced at Oren, who was sensible enough to half close his eyes and appear as nonthreatening as possible, despite the obvious size advantage he had over these people. How small were they, anyway? Oren wasn't big by Taurean standards, but it was hard to gauge just how much bigger he was while laying flat on his back.

"And, besides, unless you know something I don't, S.E.T.L. can't interrogate him if they can't communicate with him, right?" She raised an eyebrow at the man.

Oren ignored them both, pretending he did not know what was going on. The man looked pissed, then turned on his heel to leave the room, saying, "I'll be back tomorrow. They'll want them moved, whether you like it or not."

The significance of the man's words was not lost on Oren. He had said *them*. The humans must have the captured Xakul and had him in custody. If that was true, they were all in trouble. What a shit show.

Oren glanced over at Amelia, who was standing by his bed with her hands on her hips, one eyebrow raised in question. She said, "You know exactly what we're saying, don't you?"

He met her eyes and nodded.

"Well, shit. Things just got a lot more complicated. What am I supposed to do about that?"

CHAPTER FOUR

Amelia

The previous night had passed relatively uneventfully, after the initial shock of caring for an alien had worn off. It wasn't as if he had horns, or blue skin, or anything like that. Amelia had watched her patient—her *only* patient—all night. Used to a busier environment, even on this relatively quiet base, boredom had quickly set in. She had sipped on endless cups of the god-awful hospital coffee, and she had paced the room, checking the heart rate monitor regularly, realizing that an incredibly slow heart rate must be normal for him.

It had been somewhere between midnight and two am when she had an epiphany. It didn't matter who or what this man was; he was her patient and, like all her patients, she had a duty of care to make sure he was well looked after. That she did no harm. And so, with that in mind, she had snooped in the files at the nurse's station to see what she could find.

He had no chart. He had no digital file. There was nothing. It was as if he didn't exist. But the man lying in the bed in front of her was very real. From the top of his shaved head to his toes, this was a very real person. If it wasn't for his unnaturally bright eyes, he could pass as human, albeit a rather large one.

Amelia looked again at the giant on the bed. His hands were massive, the long fingers tipped with neatly trimmed nails, the palms callused and firm. Her eyes drifted over his solid forearms roped with muscle, and over biceps that bulged, and a chest that strained tightly against the largest hospital gown they could find. His golden skin in stark contrast to the bright, starched white of the cotton. He had the brawny appearance of a linebacker—he was easily as big as one, without an ounce of fat on him. If she was being honest, he had to be the most gorgeous man she had ever seen.

Her extended dry spell now stretched into months, so it was not too hard to appreciate this masculine visitor. But, best not to think about that.

All night she had wanted him to open those eyes so she could see if she had been right about the color the first time. They were not a human blue, like her own. They were unnaturally piercing and deep, almost aqua. Nobody had eyes that color. Her own blue eyes were quite pale by comparison, but still not that unusual, especially on redheads like her.

What was most interesting was that she knew he could understand her. She did not know why or how, but she knew for a fact that nothing that was said escaped him. She didn't trust the man, Major Sculder, from S.E.T.L.. He might call himself a doctor, but his notion of the Hippocratic Oath was not the same as hers. He was someone who wouldn't hesitate to drug a patient without consent. And it seemed like her colleague, James—someone she had previously trusted—felt the same way. But her commitment to that oath meant she would do what was morally right to help this patient—alien or not. She had reached another professional point of no return. She would let nothing bad happen to him, no matter what S.E.T.L. had to say.

Seeing that he was still sleeping, she left the room to get another coffee, and when she returned, he was awake. So, steeling herself to commit to something she knew would change her entire professional life, Amelia pulled up a chair next to his bed and looked him in the eye.

"You understand me, but I don't understand you."

The big alien met her gaze and smiled slightly, as if encouraging her to continue.

Amelia took his large hand in both of hers and recorded his pulse. She was surprised at the warmth she felt in his fingers. He squeezed her hand gently, running his thumb over the back of her hands.

A shiver went through her at the contact, his touch sending a flush to her cheeks. She suddenly felt as if someone had sucked all the air out of the room, and she gasped.

She released his hand and refocused. "My name is Amelia." Her tongue darted out to wet her lips, and his eyes dropped to her mouth. "What's your name?"

His deep voice sent shivers along Amelia's skin.

"Oren Ka'Ress."

"Uhren Cass?" She tried his name, the sound unfamiliar to her.

He smiled, but shook his head slowly, "Oh-ren Kah-ress."

She tried again, smiling when he nodded to show she had got it right.

"Uhmela?"

She laughed, correcting him until he could pronounce her name correctly.

They shared a smile.

"I want to know how you got here. Are you from outside our solar system?"

Oren nodded.

"What are you doing here? Are your people going to invade Earth?"

His eyes widened, and he shook his head quickly, saying something in his low, deep voice. Amelia held up her hand, and he stopped.

"Ok, so you're not here to invade us. Were you planning to come to Earth?"

A wry smile and another shake of his head.

"So," Amelia guessed, "You had an accident?"

This time, he nodded.

"Are you a soldier?"

His brows furrowed, as if not understanding the question.

"Maybe that word doesn't translate... um, are you a fighter?"

A low chuckle reached her ears as his face broke into a mesmerizing smile. It took his features from attractive to stunningly handsome, and Amelia's breath caught.

Oh, this would not do. No way. Trust her to get herself attracted to an alien! She checked her watch and realized it wasn't long until shift change.

"Oren, I don't have long until the end of my shift. I want to help you, so here's what you need to do."

He stiffened at her words, his eyes narrowing as he watched her intently. She took a deep breath and continued, "You need to pretend that you can't understand anyone. Don't let on that you know what is going on."

Oren's brows creased in concentration as he looked at her.

Amelia continued, "I don't like what's happening here, and I need more information about what is being planned for you. I'll be back tonight for my shift. Just try to rest today. As long as you stay quiet, no one will bother you. Ok?"

Oren did not look thrilled by her suggestion, but she had no other option. She could hardly stay when her shift was up. Besides, she was dead on her feet. She needed to figure out what was going on, and what S.E.T.L. had planned for Oren.

She stood, but paused as a sound from the hallway made them both hyper alert.

CHAPTER FIVE

Oren

Oren's ears cocked as the squeak of a sticky wheel marked the transit of a trolley along the long hall. Oren let his muscles relax, mindful of Amelia's warning to not let anyone know he understood them. He didn't know exactly why he trusted the red-haired woman, but he hadn't got himself out of innumerable scrapes by *not* trusting his gut. And, right now, his gut was telling him to trust Amelia, and to get the hell out of here.

He watched through half-closed eyes as a metal trolley was pushed through the open doorway. The smell of food greeted him, his stomach growling in response. How long had it been since he'd last eaten? Maybe some packaged rations a day or so ago, but with all the trouble with the ship, he hadn't thought about food. If he was to get out of here, he needed to maintain his strength. He needed to eat.

The woman pushing the trolley hesitated in the doorway, then steeled herself and pushed the trolley into the room. Her eyes widened in terror at the sight of Oren on the bed, and he suppressed a laugh. What did these people think he was going to do? Leap from the bed and begin murdering everyone?

The woman visibly relaxed when she saw Amelia in the room.

"Dr. Milly! I'm so glad you're still here. Do you think you could help...?" The woman gestured between the trolley and Oren.

Amelia raised an eyebrow at the other woman.

"I know it's not the job for a doctor, and your shift is probably almost up, but," she dropped her voice and peered around, "he's, you know..."

"He's... what?"

"Dangerous!" she hissed.

Amelia raised an eyebrow at the other woman. "He's our patient, Janet."

"Yes, I know."

Amelia sighed, and grabbing the cart, moved it towards the bed. "You owe me one, Janet."

Janet quickly left the room, throwing a hasty thank you over her shoulder as she raced out the door.

Amelia smiled, shaking her head, taking the covers off the food on the tray. The smell of hot food hit him, more intensely this time, and Oren's stomach growled again.

"Hungry,?"

Oren's eyes met hers, and he nodded.

"Alright, well don't judge Earth cuisine based on hospital food. I promise we have much better than this." Her face twisted as she picked up a fork and poked at a brown blob in a bowl.

Oren didn't think it looked or smelled very appetizing, but he was so hungry he'd eat almost anything.

"I can't undo the restraints in case the guard comes back in. I'll need to feed you myself. Is that alright?" Her eyes didn't quite meet his, and a flush stained her cheeks. She was embarrassed for him and for herself.

Her concern touched him. She differed from the other people he had met so far. He nodded his permission and smiled wryly.

"Alright, let's get you up then," she said, busying herself with the controls on the bed to change his position to upright. She grabbed a pillow and adjusted it behind his back. "Comfortable?"

Oren couldn't remember the last time someone had taken an interest in his comfort. He braced himself as he shifted slightly on the bed, steeling himself against the spear of pain the spread across his chest from his damaged ribs. What he wouldn't do right now for the most basic of Taurean medical technology. Even what he had in the small shipboard first aid kit was better than the treatment he'd received so far. He held his breath against the pain, panting as he settled into position.

"Broken ribs aren't much fun, are they?"

He shot a glance at her.

"Alright, I get it, not one for a joke. Let's see what you think of this food."

Oren turned his head to see the brown blob, now on a fork, being thrust towards his face. He grimaced.

"Amelia," he began.

"Yes?"

Oren knew she wouldn't understand, but he had to try.

"The Xakul that was on my shuttle is extremely dangerous and should be kept in a proper holding cell. I only hope you have somewhere strong enough to hold it."

Amelia frowned, "You know I can't understand you." She waved the fork of food at him again, and Oren groaned and turned his head away. He had to make her understand the serious threat the Xakul presented.

"Open wide," Amelia smirked in a singsong voice. Her joking manner made him smile, but he narrowed his eyes as he turned towards her. She wouldn't be joking around if she knew how dangerous that Xakul was.

Aware of his hunger, he opened his mouth and took a bite of the bland brown blob on the fork. There was no point in wasting time. He had to regain his strength. Eat first, and then try to get her to understand.

"It can't be that bad, surely?" Amelia continued to feed him from the tray, and Oren ate everything she offered. It was bland, unlike the spicy Taurean food he enjoyed, but it was tolerable, and he had eaten worse.

When he finished, she leaned over and held a cup of water for him. He wrapped his lips around the straw and then, meeting her eyes, sucked on the straw, his cheeks hollowing. She flushed and turned away.

Well, that was interesting, he thought to himself. She couldn't be attracted to him, could she? Oren considered that possibility and smiled around the straw. He drained the water and looked at her.

"Amelia," he said, knowing his accent was poor.

She looked at him, "Hmm?"

"I wasn't alone on my shuttle."

She knew from his expression that he was trying to tell

her something important. "I still don't know what you're saying."

He held out two long fingers.

"Two?" She stared at his hand, eyebrows drawn together.

Oren nodded. "Two."

"I'm confused. Two what?"

He stared at her, willing her to begin the game they had played before. The one where she asked questions, and he gave yes or no answers.

She sat in the chair next to his bed, positioning it so she could see the doorway. Oren nodded in approval.

"Ok. So, two. Two days?"

He shook his head.

"So, nothing to do with time?"

He shook. "No."

"Two spaceships?"

"No."

They continued for a few minutes, Amelia asking questions that became more and more outlandish as she became increasingly frustrated. She threw her hands up in the air and said the first thing that came into her mind, "I don't know. Two aliens?"

"Yes."

Her eyes widened in shock. "What, there's two of you?"

"No."

"What do you mean? You just said two aliens. So, there must be two of you."

Oren shook his head.

"Oh. So two aliens, but the other one is not like you...?" She suggested.

"Yes."

"Do you know where it is?"

"No."

"But it's here somewhere, isn't it?"

"Yes."

"Is it dangerous?"

"Yes," he said, trying his best to convey how serious the situation was with just the one word.

"Oh, shit."

CHAPTER SIX

Amelia

Night shifts always screwed with Amelia's sleep. She would arrive home as the sun rose and people, normal people who didn't work at night, were out walking their dogs and getting on with their days. She knew it was unreasonable, but she resented dog walkers and their normal lives.

She pulled into her spot at her apartment building and headed inside. It was a modest place, but she'd long since given up setting down roots. Amelia had very little to cart around. What was the point when it would just need to be packed up again in a few months? She hadn't bothered unpacking the moving boxes after her last move, and now she couldn't remember what was in them.

Amelia unlocked her door and entered her apartment. Kicking off her shoes, she wiggled her toes on the welcome cool of the tiles. She dropped her backpack on the sofa and walked into the bathroom.

As if on autopilot, she pulled off her scrubs and undid her utilitarian sports bra, letting it drop onto the floor along with her briefs. She reached into the shower and turned on the water, letting steam fill the small bathroom. She stepped into the cubicle and turned her back to the spray, allowing the hot water and steam to soothe her tired muscles.

Amelia sighed as the warmth from the water relaxed her, allowing her thoughts to drift to Oren and the revelation that he had not arrived on Earth alone. Maybe she had misunderstood? Her shift had been up, and when her replacement arrived, she had had no option but to leave and go home. Besides, the S.E.T.L. people would have the second alien locked up somewhere, if there even was one. They would keep it contained and keep everyone safe.

As she thought more about the whole situation, she was curious about why, even with all their high-tech equipment, they hadn't figured out that Oren could understand them.

But there was nothing she could do right now. She turned the water off and wrapped a towel around herself. It didn't matter either way. She had to get some rest.

Amelia made quick work of drying her hair, putting on her cotton pajamas and climbing into bed, the blackout blinds drawn against the daylight. She punched the pillow into a shape that felt comfortable and shifted around, feeling restless, her mind active.

What was the deal with these aliens? How many of these aliens were there, and where did they come from? How did they get to Earth? Oren had said that his people weren't interested in invading Earth, but what about this other species? Oren seemed very concerned about them.

————

She woke to her alarm going off, surprised that she had even fallen asleep. Amelia got out of bed and fired up her expensive Italian espresso machine—her one little luxury, and then threw on some clean scrubs and was out of the door in fifteen minutes, a double shot latte in hand.

The trip to the base was familiar, yet strange. Everything looked the same, everyone acted the same, but Amelia knew everything was changing. Nothing would ever be the same again. The radio in the Jeep played hits from the days when there was still hope for the future of the planet she called home.

She soon found herself parked outside the hospital, the setting sun lighting up the sky in shades of orange and pink. The only good thing about so much pollution in the atmosphere was the spectacular sunsets.

As Amelia walked towards the concrete and glass building, she wondered what Oren's day had been like. Had he slipped up and given away that could understand everything that was being said? She hoped not. Reaching her locker, she put her bag inside and made her way to the cafeteria on the ground level to grab a breakfast sandwich.

The room was mostly empty, except for one server and a few hospital workers. Amelia saw Janet and, grabbing her food, made her way over to join her.

"Hi, Janet."

"Oh, hi Dr. Milly," Janet's greeting wasn't as enthusiastic as usual.

Though Amelia found her irritating at times, she didn't dislike the woman, so she asked, "Is everything ok?"

A small sigh was Janet's reply, as she stared at her coffee cup and fiddled with the rim. "It just feels like every day is the same old thing. I thought I'd be doing more here, you know?"

That same feeling was all too familiar to Amelia. "Like what?" she asked.

"You know the recruitment ads? The ones with the spaceships and the promises of going to Mars? Of being the first people to colonize the new planet?"

Amelia took a bite of her sandwich and nodded.

"I wanted that. That's why I signed up." Janet's face had lost its usual animation.

Amelia made a spur-of-the-moment decision and reached out to pat Janet's hand reassuringly. "It's not all bad. I have a feeling that soon things won't be so boring around here."

"Really?" Janet's eyebrows drew down in confusion.

"I dunno. I have a feeling that not everything is as it seems." Amelia looked at her watch and got up from the table and said, "Sorry, I've got to get going. Have a good day," leaving the confused nurse behind.

As she walked towards the doorway, the conversation of a pair of orderlies caught her attention.

"... some weird shit on him, hey?"

"Yeah."

"What is it all for? All those gadgets... and his clothes? I ain't seen nothing like it!"

Amelia stiffened, slowing as she passed the table.

"Those S.E.T.L. weirdos really have a hard-on for him, don't they?"

"Yeah, good thing he's being moved in the morning. It's been a nightmare trying to manage everyone with that whole ward closed off."

Amelia avoided their eyes and walked towards the elevator. Her heart beat faster. They had to be speaking about Oren. So, where *was* his stuff? She rode the elevator up to the ward, determined to find out more.

Amelia swiped her pass through the various security checkpoints and, a short while later, was standing in the doorway to Oren's room. She was reminded again of just how big he was. His hospital gown had been removed, his torso only partially covered by the blanket, his arms and legs still restrained to the sides of the bed. Amelia jumped as a voice came from behind her.

"He wouldn't let us put another gown on him, even drugged up as he was."

Amelia turned and recognized a nurse she had worked with before.

"Oh? Do you need some help?"

"Yeah, he's a big dude, and if he doesn't want to do something..." The nurse shrugged.

Inspiration struck Amelia, and she spoke without thinking, "Yeah, I get what you mean. Hey, he's being moved in the morning, right? Maybe if he had the things he arrived with, he might be easier to motivate." She cringed inwardly at how that sounded.

"That's a good idea. I think they took his stuff down to the nurses' station. I'll go check."

"Thanks," Amelia smiled as the nurse left. Turning back to the bed, she found Oren's eyes focused on her with laser-like intensity.

"Yeah, yeah, I know what you are thinking. But you want your stuff back, don't you?"

He nodded slowly.

"Well, that's what you get for listening to other people's conversations." She approached the bed and grinned at him, his lips twitching in reply. He opened his mouth, as if to say something, but quickly snapped his jaw shut and relaxed, as if asleep, his eyes closing. Amelia was confused for a second until she heard footsteps in the hallway. How good was his hearing, anyway? That was freaky.

She turned to see the nurse bring a box into the room, its lid perched precariously on top.

"That was quick." Amelia accepted the box and, dismissing the nurse, turned to place it on a chair next to Oren's bed.

"Alright. Let's see what you have in here."

"Amelia," Oren's deep voice sent a shiver through her.

"Hmm?" She kept her head down as she pulled the largest pair of boots she had ever seen from the box and put them on the floor.

Oren spoke again, repeating a word in his language over and over.

"Ok, let's figure out what you want." Amelia said as she began fishing around in the box.

CHAPTER SEVEN

Oren

"Communicator," Oren repeated the word again as he pointed a finger at an object in Amelia's hand.

"This?" She held up his comm, the square device attached to a band that he wore wrapped around his wrist.

He nodded, and she brought it over to him. His hands were still strapped to the bed, but, with a resigned sigh, Amelia unstrapped his wrists from the bed.

"Don't make me regret doing this," she muttered under her breath.

He smiled and touched a finger to her cheek, feeling the smooth skin under his calloused hand. This doctor had kept his racing thoughts focused. Amelia could understand him. She had taken the time to observe and understand him. It was as if she had seen through him a feeling that should make him very uncomfortable, considering what he did. Those who worked in Taurean intelligence lived and worked on the periphery, never spending enough time on any one starship to forge lasting relationships.

He shifted on the bed, grimacing. Every slight movement hurt, the bruised ribs making him wish, not for the first time, for his own medical technology. He forced himself to relax and breathe deeply. The familiar pain of a rib injury was, although not exactly welcome, at least a distraction from his racing thoughts.

Amelia watched his face and offered the unresponsive comm.

Oren took it from her and smiled in thanks. Turning his attention to the device, he tapped the screen. Nothing. The screen was blank.

"Fuck! Just what I need."

He spent some minutes fiddling with it, trying all the simple tricks he knew to restart the small device.

"Is the battery dead?" Amelia asked.

He looked up at Amelia's soft enquiry, realizing how close their heads were as she leaned over to see the comm. She pushed back an errant curl that had escaped the mass tied up on top of her head, ignoring it as it slipped forwards again to fall across her cheek. Their eyes met and held. Oren's heart beat faster in his chest as he reached up to finger the soft lock.

"I'll go get a charging pad. You never know, it might work." Amelia spun on her heel and rushed from the room, leaving him blinking in surprise.

Oren did not know what a charging pad was, but if it got his comm working, then it was worth giving it a go. He needed to talk to Amelia about the Xakul. He had to impress upon her the urgency of controlling the lone soldier.

... And he had to get off this planet.

He had secured the Xakul captive in the hold of his ship and, before he'd lost consciousness, he'd checked to make sure it was secure after the crash. Surely his captors wouldn't have been so stupid as to release it? Oren shuddered at the thought of the Xakul soldier being released on an unprepared population.

The Xakul were hideous, even more so when seeing them in battle mode. Six legs spread over three segments propelled them faster than any bipedal species could hope to travel. When standing on their back legs, they towered over Oren, and he was not a short Taurean, almost seven feet tall. He had always found their many eyes disturbing, and that was before you got to the pincers, that were brutally efficient at tearing apart their prey.

And tear apart they did.

Before turning to intelligence gathering, Oren had spent a few years in the Taurean infantry. He had seen his fair share of terrible things on the battlefield, but swarming Xakul were definitely the worst.

This one Xakul soldier might not be part of a swarm, but Oren had seen the human weapons, and they were unlikely to take down a Xakul in battle mode. Hell, who was he trying to kid? They wouldn't be able to take one down if it did half the work for them! The Xakul's natural armor, that formed their exoskeleton, was impervious to all but the most advanced plasma projectiles. And in close combat? Forget about it, unless you had a laser saber. Only a weapon with an electrified blade would stop a mature

Xakul soldier. He shuddered to think what an army of Xakul soldiers could do to this planet.

He really had to get his comm working. Amelia deserved to know what was coming, to know what to prepare for. His comm would translate his Taurean language into her language so they could communicate more efficiently. Right now he was relying on every gesture, every touch, every lift of an eyebrow, to help her understand him. Under different circumstances, it would have been a welcome distraction.

Who was he trying to fool? He was all but drowning in her kind, blue gaze and gentle touch. He was completely distracted!

The woman herself returned, coming back into the room holding something in her hand. She fumbled against the wall at the head of the bed and then placed a small black device on the table nearby.

"Give me the watch," she held out her hand, and he placed his comm in her outstretched fingers. She put it on the rectangle and watched it intently.

Nothing happened.

"Oh. I thought it might work." The disappointment in her voice touched Oren, and he reached to entangle his fingers in hers and squeezed gently to show he understood her frustration.

"I didn't join this stupid organisation to hurt people, you know?" She laughed humorlessly.

Oren brushed his thumb back and forth over her hand, her fingers gripping his tightly. He knew exactly what Amelia meant. His own time in the Taurean military had not been what he had expected. The pride he had felt was still there, but he was no longer the naïve young warrior, determined to prove himself.

That's why intelligence suited Oren so well. Living his life on the periphery and letting others take the glory was fine with him. During the infrequent times he returned to Taurus to visit his family, he did not wear his uniform, preferring to blend into the crowds of civilians rather than stand out with all his rank and regalia. Not that he wasn't proud of who he was and what he did, it was just that he wanted people to know that there was more to him than just his job.

"I wish we could talk properly. There's so much that I want to know." Amelia's soft voice jerked him back to the present.

He smiled, "Me too."

He had so many questions. Where exactly was he? He knew the planet was called Earth, with a sentient space faring race, but with the AI out of action, and Oren battling to control the ship, he had had no time to investigate further. He had crash-landed with no idea what he had gotten himself into.

A beeping noise caught his attention, and he turned as Amelia gasped.

"It's working!" Her smile was so bright he couldn't help but return it.

She picked up the comm, the screen now lit up, and handed it to him. "Here's your watch. It's kind of weird that you have all this advanced technology in a standard wrist watch."

Oren laughed, turning his attention to the comm and quickly cycling through the settings until he found the one he wanted. He made a selection and then, strapping the comm to his wrist, turned to Amelia.

"That's because it's not a watch," he stared at her as the comm translated Taurean into her language, willing her to recognize what he had said. It did not disappoint him when her eyes went wide.

"Well, great! It works!"

CHAPTER EIGHT

Amelia

It worked! It actually worked! And she could understand him! She stared at him for a moment, her mind completely blank as she took in his self-satisfied smile, his broad arms now crossed over his chest. He might be the one lying in the hospital bed, but she felt at a decided disadvantage.

Amelia quickly walked to the door into the hallway and, checking to make sure there was nobody outside, eased the door closed. She returned to the bed, stopping at the foot and watching him with her head tilted to one side.

"Alright, so you're not from Earth. I figured out that much, at least."

He took a while to answer, brows drawn together in consideration, as if trying to work out how much to tell her.

"No, I'm not."

"Alright," Amelia knew he wasn't from here, but part of her had held onto the hope that it had all been some big mistake. She hoped the looming feeling that her life was about to be turned upside down would be an unjustified worry. But it looked like that was not the case.

"Why did you come to Earth?"

A bark of laughter escaped him, and he rolled his eyes. He actually rolled his eyes! The movement that Amelia attributed to teenage girls looked so out of place on Oren that it made her laugh.

"It wasn't on purpose, believe me. I incurred some damage to my spaceship and needed to stop until I could get picked up."

"Picked up... how?"

He shifted on his bed, lifting the watch to tap at the screen. "Some friends are dropping by to get me."

"You make it sound like they'll just walk right in."

He didn't bother to reply, just looked pointedly at her.

"Oh, right. I get it. They will, won't they? Just walk right in?"

He nodded slowly.

"Huh." She busied her hands with the blanket, smoothing a rumple in the thick cotton as if it would smooth the waves of rising panic she felt.

"Amelia, I wasn't alone on that spaceship."

The way her name sounded in his deep voice momentarily distracted her, but then she realized what he hadn't said. Her eyes snapped to his. "What? What do you mean? Who else was with you?"

"Not *who* else, but *what* else."

Amelia's eyes widened. How could she have forgotten about the second alien?

"Xakul," he spat out.

Amelia attempted to repeat it, the guttural first syllable foreign to her tongue. "I don't understand." She felt as if the world had tilted off its axis, throwing everything she knew and understood into disarray.

Oren grimaced. "They are a race determined to destroy habitable planets and use them as nurseries for their own young. They take over and lay their eggs. When they hatch, the young consume everything in sight, including any inhabitants. Only the strongest, most brutal young survive, becoming soldiers."

"What?" Amelia started laughing. It sounded absolutely ridiculous. Oren was not laughing, and she sobered. "Oh, my god. You're not kidding. You're dead serious. No way."

Shaking her head, Amelia backed away from the bed. "This is insane. You're insane. This is all some giant joke, and I'm not falling for it."

Amelia turned and bolted from the room, needing some distance to consider what Oren had just said. She was thankful that he did not follow her, which he could have done since she had unstrapped his hands from the bed. She was an idiot, and he was a complete madman.

Surely, if they had encountered sentient alien life, she would have heard about it? A thought niggled at the back of her mind. But really, how much had she been told about Oren, besides nothing? She had made assumptions, but actually hadn't been told anything concrete. She needed to find out what the hell was going on.

Decision made, Amelia walked quickly down the hallway and away from Oren's room. She reached the security doors that led out of the ward and lifted her access card to swipe the security panel. Then she heard a voice from behind a partially closed office door, and she listened.

"It's not as if we can do anything about it right now, Sir."

Then there was a pause.

"Of course, but—"

Amelia identified the voice as that of, Major Sculder, the S.E.T.L. doctor she had met the first day Oren had arrived. He was on a phone call.

"Of the two of them, the humanoid one is the better bet for information, yes."

So there were two aliens on this base. She knew where Oren was, but what about the second one?

"Yes, it's secured in the basement holding cells. That's the best place we have right now. We don't know what its physiology is like. I'm not a xenobiologist... or a veterinarian!"

The man cursed and Amelia jumped, quickly turning to swipe her card and exit through the ward doors. She walked on autopilot to the staff lounge, grabbing a coffee mug and filling it. She took a sip of the scalding hot liquid, the familiar movements calming her.

She thought of Oren. He had been intense when he had matter-of-factly told her he was not from Earth, and that there was another being with him when he crashed his spaceship. Spaceship! Unbelievable.

Humans were not alone in the universe. They had proven that there was other sentient life out there. It was the discovery of the millennium! People on the planet would want to see this alien for themselves and find out what his life had been like.

Every person on the planet.

Amelia felt sick. Oren had a life. He was injured right now, but he had a life to get back to. For all she knew, he might have a family who missed him, a job. Who knew what life was like on his home planet?

But that other alien, that Xakul soldier Oren had with him on his spaceship. The disdain with which he referred to it spoke volumes. It was dangerous, but she needed to know what it was like. Amelia cursed her curiosity. Life would be so much easier if she didn't need to know everything. She needed to see this Xakul for herself.

She rinsed out her coffee cup and, nodding to the few colleagues taking a break during their long night shifts, she headed to the basement level.

She walked briskly, but did not want to appear rushed. Even though there were few people around, she did not want to draw undue attention to herself.

The lift, as usual, creaked and groaned; the old building protesting as she descended many levels below ground. The actual basement itself was well below ground level, and was much cooler than the upper levels.

Amelia stepped off the lift and turned toward the holding cells. She had never actually been to them before. The supply stores were in the basement, but in the opposite direction, and she had no real reason to be down here. If anyone asked her what she was doing, she would say that she was just popping down for some medical supplies. She rolled her eyes at herself. As if anyone would believe that excuse. A nurse or an orderly would normally come down for supplies, not a doctor. She hoped she wouldn't run into anyone.

A loud shout reached her as she turned the corner that

led to the holding cells. Two large double doors indicated the entry point. These were usually wide open, at least whenever Amelia had seen them, but today were shut and locked, the swipe pad lit up in bright red, signaling "no entry". She walked to the doors and peered through the glass pane into the wing that held the holding cells.

The room beyond the doors acted as a guard station, separating the holding cells from the general access area. A large metal grille, spanning floor to ceiling, separated the guard station from the cells proper. Amelia lifted onto her toes, straining to see through the glass.

She jumped when a second, louder shout spilled into the corridor.

Smoke filled the far end of the hallway where the cells were located, the overhead lights flickering and giving the space an ominous feeling. Amelia realized it wasn't smoke, but a white gas that filled most of the hallway. A smear of something red on the ground caught her attention. It looked like blood. Amelia felt sick, blinking in disbelief as her eyes focused on the dismembered body of what must have been a guard. A leg, still wearing fatigue pants and a combat boot, lay in the hallway, blood spreading across the floor. She swallowed hard, heart pumping, pushing down the bile that rose in her throat.

What was happening here?

She could see a second guard further along the hallway, his back to Amelia, feet braced as he raised his weapon to his shoulder. He shouted, his words muffled. Amelia squinted as a shape loomed through the gas beyond the guard. She shivered as the hair on the back of her neck lifted, goosebumps spreading over her skin. She shook her head and blinked to clear her vision, straining to focus.

Then, with inhuman speed, the shape lunged at the guard. The retort of his weapon was deafening. Amelia pressed her hands to her ears and squeezed her eyes shut. Her heart beat frantically and some sense of self-preservation made her eyes fly open.

She peered through the glass panel in the door once more. It took a few moments before she could reconcile what she was seeing. It was as if her eyes had passed the information to her brain, but her brain didn't want to comprehend it.

There was no sign of the second guard. Standing where the guard had stood was a giant insect, but unlike anything Amelia had ever seen. Its body was dark, the light playing off its exoskeleton like oil on water. The colors would be beautiful, if it wasn't so horrifying. It stood erect on four legs; two more raised in front of it like arms. Its head had antennae that moved this way and that, as if trying to sense what was in the surrounding space.

Amelia gasped, and the antenna stopped moving, turning to point towards her with laser-like focus. She stumbled backwards, but not before the head of the insect, covered with thousands of small eyes, had turned to pierce her with its gaze.

She turned and ran.

CHAPTER NINE

Oren

Oren was used to working alone, used to being the strong one and getting himself out of trouble. Maybe this time he needed to swallow his pride and accept help? The thought wasn't as abhorrent as he expected... not when it came from Amelia.

He had called out to her after she'd rushed from the room, but she hadn't returned. Something must be wrong. She should have returned by now. He had to get out of this room and find her.

A frustrated noise escaped Oren's lips as he shifted, testing the restraints holding his feet to the bed. He was unused to feeling this weak pain pulsing through his chest with every movement, and the sedatives he had been given making his head swim. Sweat beaded his brow as he reached forwards to undo the thick fabric straps. He grunted in exertion, the muscles in his neck pulsing as he gritted his teeth. He undid one, then the other and, finally free, he flopped back on the bed, gasping for breath.

This was almost comical. What he wouldn't do for Taurean medical care right now.

He needed to keep calm. The only saving grace was that Domik wasn't here. And if Oren had his way, his brother would never hear about this. The two had a friendly rivalry going, and Domik would take any opportunity to tease his older brother. Oren shook his head.

Where the hell was Amelia? He knew she had been shocked. It had been a lot to take in. As an intelligence officer, he could not share much of what he did with anyone. It made personal relationships difficult, and the irony of him finally telling someone the truth and having it backfire in his face...? Yeah, he wasn't about to live this one down.

He eased his feet over the side of the bed and sat up, bracing himself as the room spun. Taking deep breaths, he waited until the dizziness passed and then stood, holding onto the side of the bed before reaching for the box Amelia had brought into the room.

Rummaging around, he pulled out his pants and shirt. It took some minutes to dress, Oren becoming frustrated as his limbs did not respond as quickly as he expected them to. How long would it take for these drugs to get out of his system?

When he finally had his pants on, he sat in the chair Amelia had used, his broad frame barely fitting, and bent to pull on his boots.

A distant sound caught Oren's attention, and he

stiffened and stilled his movements, straining to listen for any further noises.

He was used to cataloguing the normal daily routines of others. It was when something abnormal stuck out that his sixth sense came to the fore. And now? That sixth sense was telling him that something was definitely wrong.

A distant door slammed, followed by a scream.

Where the *hell* was Amelia?

Oren rushed to finish pulling on his boots and stood, bracing himself on the back of the chair as black spots appeared in his vision.

His eyes shot to the doorway as he heard the telltale sound of a scanner pad in the hallway beeping as someone entered the ward. Oren swore and, as quickly as his injured body would allow, made his way to the door, flattening himself against the wall, out of sight.

His heartbeat thudded in his ears as he readied himself, wishing he still had his plasma pistol. The small weapon was perfect for situations like these when you might need a weapon, but didn't want to draw any attention. No point in worrying about that now. At least he was bigger than most of the humans he'd seen. Even in his weakened state, he could probably overpower them if he took them by surprise, but if there were more than one or two, he might be in trouble.

Oren strained to listen to the footsteps. Was that only one person? They were running, and it certainly sounded like only one person. Their tread was light. Was it Amelia?

With the squeak of the soles of shoes sliding on linoleum, a small hand wrapped itself around the doorway and the woman herself shot into the room, curly red hair flying around her head like it had a life of its own.

She skidded to a halt, not noticing Oren against the wall, as she took in the empty bed.

"Fuck!" The word filled the stark white room, bouncing off the walls.

"Looking for me?" Oren asked, and she gasped, spinning on her heel, eyes wide in shock as she looked up at him.

"You shouldn't be out of bed," she reprimanded him, and then shook her head. "Forget that. We have to get out of here."

Oren raised an eyebrow, "I gathered that."

"That... that *thing*. It..." she threw a hand in the air and gestured wildly.

"What did you see, Amelia?" Oren was immediately all business, reaching a hand towards her, palm outwards, as if to calm her down. Amelia stared at his hand, eyes wide.

"I saw the other alien," she whispered softly. "And it saw me."

"Fuck!" If the Xakul had seen Amelia, then the hunt was on. It would track her down until either she or it was dead. She was right; they had to get out of there. The human's weapons were no match for the Xakul.

"Can you get us out of here?" Oren asked, sliding a finger under her chin and tilting her head so their eyes met. Her eyes were enormous.

"What about all the people? There were so many already dead." Her eyes stared over his shoulder, unfocused. "Oh, god. Janet!" Her already pale skin lost even more color.

"Amelia." Oren's firm voice had Amelia's eyes snapping to his face. "Is there an alarm?"

"Of course! The fire alarm." Amelia turned to the doorway and raced into the hall. A few seconds later, Oren heard a telltale sound of glass breaking and then an alarm droned.

She skidded back into the room. "Hopefully that will get people out." Amelia's words were a little shaky, but now that she had something to do, she seemed more purposeful.

"Alright, let's go."

It didn't take him long to realize that, without Amelia's help, he would not make it out of the building. She found a wheelchair and together they made it out of the ward and to the bank of elevators.

"Something isn't right." Amelia's words felt ominous as they waited for the elevator to arrive. When the doors opened, she gagged at the sight that greeted them. The body of an orderly lay on the floor, blood pooled around him, a bloody handprint on the wall next to the controls.

"Is there another way out of here besides the elevator?" Oren's voice seemed to jolt through Amelia, her hands jerking on the handles of the chair.

"Only the stairs."

"Then, let's go."

Amelia set the brake on the wheelchair and moved to help Oren stand. Looping a hand around his waist, they made their way towards the stairwell next to the lifts. Amelia pushed the door open and held it for Oren as he shuffled through, breathing hard.

"Are you alright?" He asked, brows drawn in concern.

"What? Yes. No... I don't know." She rubbed a hand over her face as they stood on the concrete landing.

Oren peered over the railing. "It looks clear down there. Let's go."

They made their way, painstakingly slowly, down the stairwell. Their movements echoed against the concrete and steel, sounding conspicuously loud. They paused frequently whenever they heard a shout or running feet.

They made it down the first flight of stairs to the first landing, stopping to catch their breath. Oren peered over the railing again and, turning to Amelia, held up two fingers and raised an eyebrow in question, as if to ask if there were two more flights of stairs to negotiate. She nodded.

Breathing hard at the exertion, he looped his arm once more over Amelia's shoulder and held onto the railing, easing himself down one stair at a time.

They had almost reached the ground floor, one level above the basement, when they heard a door open above them. Amelia and Oren paused, staring up and listening intently. The eerie screech that filled the stairwell was something that Oren, unfortunately, recognized. The Xakul soldier was hot on their heels.

Amelia froze. Oren yanked on her arm, giving up all pretence of stealth, and led them thundering down the last few stairs. He pulled on the door handle, pushing Amelia through the gap before following her as a second screech sounded. Bile rose in the back of Oren's throat at the exertion and he swallowed the bitter taste, fighting to keep himself upright.

The door slammed shut behind them, cutting off the sounds of the Xakul soldier, and Oren and Amelia looked around at a scene from a horror movie.

CHAPTER TEN

Amelia

Amelia grabbed Oren's arm to stay upright.

"Oh no, oh my god," Amelia kept repeating over and over, transfixed by the sight in front of her. She felt firm fingers on her face, and then she turned to meet piercing blue eyes.

"You're alright, Amelia. Listen to me. We need to get out of here. Which way do we go?" His deep, slow voice calmed her, and she lifted a shaky hand to point towards a set of doors.

"Through there."

"Let's go."

This time she let him lead her, lending him her support despite their size difference. They stumbled amongst the debris of overturned gurneys, spilled supplies, and the occasional pool of blood. A set of keys on a lanyard lay on the floor near the supine body of a person Amelia had no hope of identifying. She shuddered, turning away.

Move. They had to move.

Her world narrowed to placing one foot in front of the other, Oren's massive form leaning on her, causing her to stumble, barely catching herself.

Reaching the doors, she pushed against them, her movements becoming frantic when they wouldn't open. All she could think of was the safety of her Jeep parked in the car park on the other side of the foyer. It was so close, but she couldn't get to it.

"Amelia, your security card?"

"Oh, right." She had been so caught up in fright she hadn't thought to swipe her card against the scanner pad. With a beep, the doors opened, and she stumbled into the foyer filled with the refreshingly frigid night air.

Amelia's shoulders relaxed slightly as they stumbled out past the chaos of tumbled chairs and discarded belongings, and into the night. She had not seen a single person, at least not anyone alive, since she had gone back to get Oren. Amelia hoped everyone had evacuated in time.

They stumbled down the steps and towards the car park, picking up the pace as they moved rapidly towards her Jeep parked in a pool of light cast by a streetlight. It had always made Amelia feel secure to park in this spot, under the light, but now she felt exposed.

Her heart raced as she moved to the passenger side and reached for the door latch. Locked.

"Shit! My keys!" She looked back at the hospital entranceway, feeling sick at the thought of going back for her keys.

Oren flicked a few things on his watch, what he called a

comm she remembered, and waved it over the door latch. Then he pulled, and the door opened.

"What...?" She looked at him in stunned relief, and he grinned.

"Will that turn on the ignition as well?"

He nodded, and she could have cried in relief. She helped him into the car and then raced around to the driver's side and jumped in, quickly hitting the electric start button. The Jeep roared to life.

Movement caught her eye through the windscreen, and she looked up at the entrance to the hospital as the doors shattered, glass spraying outwards into the night like confetti.

"Fuck! Shit! Fuck!" She threw the jeep into drive and shot out of the space and onto the road leading away from the hospital.

Oren was talking into his comm as Amelia shot a look at him.

"... being chased by a single Xakul soldier... copy... negative... yeah, yeah, Domik will love that... copy... rendezvous in three minutes... out."

The exchange sounded so human that Amelia did a double take.

"What's going on?" She shot a look into the rearview mirror, slowing to a safer speed.

"My pickup crew will meet us shortly. They're tracking me, so we just need to find a piece of open ground for them to land." He smiled across at her.

"As easy as that?"

She should feel traumatized by what she had seen. That

would probably come later, but right now she was just elated to be out of the hospital.

Oren peered in the side mirror, muttering, "Maybe not so easy after all."

Amelia checked the rear-view mirror and started at the outline of a large shape, chasing them at high speed. "What is that?" She asked, knowing the answer, but not wanting to hear it.

"Faster, go!" Oren commanded, and Amelia put her foot down, tearing her eyes away from the sight of the Xakul soldier scurrying after them at a speed she could not comprehend. Down on all six legs, it moved so fast that the legs were a blur.

"This road doesn't go forever, Oren!"

Amelia was frantic, her voice squeaking in fright. Oren's large hand settled on her thigh, reassuring her as she pushed the vehicle to its limits. The dark night whipped past, cold air streaming through a window she didn't remember opening, her hair flying about her face.

"It's OK, it's just a bit further."

The headlights of the Jeep lit up the desert, the road empty except for them and the Xakul that was still there in the rear-view mirror. Had it actually gotten closer?

The perimeter of the compound and the guard hut loomed ahead, and Amelia didn't hesitate when she reached the boom gate.

"Hold on!" She shouted, throwing an arm up in front of her face as she hit the boom gate, breaking it into pieces and shooting past. The Jeep spun sideways, the wheels squealing as they hit the turn for the highway.

Shooting across the empty lanes, the highway stretched before them, the flat desert landscape lit by the headlights of Amelia's jeep, the clouds hiding the not-quite full moon from sight.

"Shit! Can this thing go any faster?" Oren was turned in his seat, peering out the back window.

"I'm going as fast as I can!" Amelia pushed the accelerator flat to the floor, the small four-wheel-drive engine complaining at the treatment. She glanced in the side mirror, swallowing a gasp as the Xakul soldier. It was gaining on them.

Amelia dragged her eyes back to the road in front of them, cresting a slight rise. The wheels left the road for a brief second, and her stomach leaped. She clutched the steering wheel tightly, knuckles white in fright. The next moment, all four wheels landed back on the ground with a bang and the car lurched slightly, Amelia fighting for control.

Oren's large hand reached across to cover hers on the steering wheel. "Easy, you're doing great." The calm words helped settle her frantic breathing, and she forced herself to focus on the road once more.

Oren's hand left hers and he barked into the comm on his wrist, "Anytime now would be great, Zac."

A long stretch of highway spread across the valley in front of them, a single set of headlights visible in the distance, the only other vehicle in sight. Thank god for that.

Then chaos descended.

A roar of wind hit the Jeep, dust and debris flying around them, reducing the visibility to almost nothing. The smell of ozone hit her nostrils. Amelia blinked hard to clear her vision. And a blast unlike anything she had ever seen or heard shook the ground behind them.

Oren's hand reached out to her arm, gently squeezing. "You can stop now. Help is here. It's over."

CHAPTER ELEVEN

Oren

Oren's hand tightened, as if trying to push strength into her. She jolted, but her foot lifted from the accelerator and the car slowed.

"It's gone? Are you sure?" Her words escaped in a panicked rush.

"Yes, I'm sure. Zac has T'arq with him, who is one hell of a pilot, and an excellent shot."

Amelia shot a startled glance at Oren, and he smiled in what he hoped was a reassuring way. "You're safe." He didn't add the rest of the sentence: *'at least for now'*. It was enough that she had endured everything so far. She was obviously a strong woman. She had handled the situation with remarkable strength and fortitude.

Amelia pulled the jeep to a stop in the middle of the highway, engaging the handbrake and turning off the engine. She turned in her seat to face Oren.

"What just happened?" She rubbed at her eyes before

turning to open the car door and jump to the ground, not waiting for an answer.

Oren did the same, easing his big frame from the car, and shuffled towards the rear of the car where Amelia stood, hands to her face, eyes wide.

Oren followed her gaze. There was now a large, melted mass of black tar on the road, the bitumen melted into lumps that still sizzled in places. A crater marked the spot where the Taurean ship's plasma cannon had blasted the Xakul soldier. Nothing remained, not unless you counted small bits of the insect-like creature that were now spread across the road and into the desert.

Oren's nose wrinkled. As often as he had seen the impacts of plasma weapons, the smell of ozone and burning in the aftermath was something he had never gotten used to.

He slipped an arm around Amelia's shaking shoulders, pulling her to his chest in an instinctive need to comfort her. She relaxed against him, still shaking but breathing a little more steadily.

"It's gone. What did that?" She gestured towards the crater. Her troubled eyes lifted to meet his, and he lifted a hand to brush a stray curl back from her face.

"We did."

Her eyebrows drew together in confusion, and she opened her mouth as if to speak, but Oren cut her off, gesturing to the night sky.

They watched as the compact Taurean spaceship slowly drew close and lowered onto the empty road between them and the crater. It was one of the stealth craft based on Starship Zataras, where Oren was stationed. It was like his own shuttle, but designed for short missions, unlike his longer-range craft. Or what was left of his spaceship, anyway. He sighed. That was going to take some explaining.

"How can it be so quiet?" Amelia asked, drawing Oren's attention back to her.

"Noise dampeners. Do you not have them?"

She shook her head.

The streamlined rectangular craft settled easily on extended legs, and a ramp lowered from the back. Before it had hit the ground, a heavily armed form leaped from the ramp and strode towards where Oren and Amelia stood next to the Jeep. A second figure waited until the ramp had fully extended, then he descended to stand at the bottom of the ramp.

"Domik," Oren smiled in greeting at his younger brother.

"Trust you to need me to rescue you, old man." The joking tone was at odds with Domik's expression, and Oren barked a laugh, releasing Amelia and reaching out to hug his younger, but bigger, brother. The two men touched their foreheads together in the traditional Taurean greeting between close friends and family.

"Good to see you, too."

Domik reached out awkwardly with one arm, holding his plasma rifle in the other. He was clad in dark gray body armor, and had all manner of weapons strapped to his uniform, making it difficult to return Oren's embrace.

A small cough from behind him reminded Oren of Amelia's presence and he gestured towards her.

"Domik, this is Dr. Amelia O'Malley who has been

helping me." He smiled softly at her, their eyes meeting briefly.

Domik made a fist with his hand and held it to his chest. Amelia glanced between Oren and Domik, her eyebrows raised, and then, tentatively, she mimicked the gesture. "Nice to meet you, Domik."

The Taurean who had waited at the bottom of the ramp now approached, speaking into his own comm as he did so. He was taller and broader than Oren, but not as large as Domik, and he was not armed with a plasma rifle, though he wore various knives around his body.

"Zac," Oren greeted him, fist to chest. The other man nodded and repeated the gesture.

"Let's get out of here. We need to clean up this mess and get you to medical." Zac turned, Amelia glimpsing his face as he did so. She drew in a surprised breath, the sound soft but audible. Zac stiffened and paused before quickly turning away and striding back to the spaceship. One side of his face was deeply scared, his features almost unrecognizable. An angry scar twisted the skin from temple to chin.

"I'm sorry. I didn't mean..." Amelia trailed off.

"He's sensitive about the scars. He won't talk about them."

"Oh," she said in a quiet voice, then looked up at Oren. "So, I suppose this is it?"

"I suppose it is." Oren, bracing his hand against the Jeep, reached down to lift her chin with a gentle hand. Ever so slowly, he lowered his head until their foreheads touched, staring into her expressive blue eyes, filled with want and worry.

"Somehow, I don't think this will be the last time we will see each other," he spoke softly, as if trying to keep the bubble that surrounded them intact for just a few moments longer.

A throat clearing had them both jerk apart, breathing hard. Oren itched to wipe the amused smirk from Domik's face, but then his brother spoke.

"Ah, seems we have company." He gestured with a large hand to the flotilla of helicopters that were rapidly approaching.

"Oh, great," Amelia muttered, recognizing the craft.

Oren turned to her, his brows raised in question.

"What's the bet that they will blame me for all this?" She gestured to the crater and the Taurean spaceship.

CHAPTER TWELVE

Amelia

The rotors on the helicopter finally settled and Space Force marines spilled out, followed by the swaggering figure of someone who Amelia recognized as General Maximilian Russell.

Great. Just great.

She was still reeling from being chased by the Xakul warrior, and now and the biggest asshole in the whole of Space Force was headed her way. Couldn't she just have a few minutes to gather her thoughts?

Apparently not.

Oren stiffened, picking up on her distress, and eased her behind him, Domik moving to stand on her other side.

Were they protecting her?

She stared up at the two Taurean warriors. Amelia had thought Oren was massive, but the size of his brother, Domik, who was almost a head taller, completely blew her away. The large Taurean was armed to the teeth, shifting an enormous gun in his hands and, if not quite aiming it at the approaching marines, at least had it ready.

General Russell was either an idiot, or supremely confident, and everything that Amelia had heard about him suggested the latter. He strode right up to them, only stopping a few feet away.

"I believe we owe you an apology, Commander Ka'Ress," he said, addressing Oren.

Oren did not answer, instead crossing his arms over his chest and rocking his weight back and forth on his heels.

"My name is General Russell. When I heard of your capture by S.E.T.L. forces, I came as quickly as I could. I see that you already... took care of... things," he shot a pointed look at the melted road and the crater where the Xakul soldier had been blown sky high.

"What do you want?"

Amelia gasped at Oren's words. They were unexpected; nobody spoke to the General like that. But, then again, she supposed Oren had a lot to be pissed off about. Being held captive and drugged, for starters.

Russell only smiled, apparently nonplussed at Oren's tone. "Your Supreme Commander has been in contact with our Space Force leadership to arrange for your release with apology."

Oren snorted in disgust.

A bitter smile spread across the General's face as he took a step closer. Domik's hands moved subtly to his weapon, which was not lost on the old Space Force marine.

"What could we want with you?" Domik could contain himself no longer.

Not sparing a look at Domik, Russell answered the question, eyes still on Oren. "It's not what you want with us," he said, pausing before continuing, "but what Earth and Taurus both need and want."

"And that is what, exactly, sir?" This time it was Amelia who asked, stepping out from behind Oren.

"Ah, the doctor. You did well to get Commander Ka'Ress out when that Xakul soldier went wild."

"Thank you, sir, but, with all due respect, what the hell is going on?" Amelia's normally calm nature had been pushed to the limits.

For the first time, General Russell lost his composure and, rubbing a hand over his face, he suddenly looked exhausted.

"There was an attack on Mars by the Xakul."

Amelia gasped, her hand covering her mouth in shock. Having seen for herself the terror and destruction even one Xakul warrior could create; she knew the immediate situation was dire.

"The only reason it wasn't a complete annihilation is because the Starship Zataras was in the area and Commander Ka'Ress here could assist. They scared off most of the attack force, but it was a little too late for one colony." He paused, his face showing strain and fatigue.

Amelia felt the blood rush from her face. The colonies on Mars were supposed to be the hope for humanity's future. The terraforming projects—growing food and building a habitable planet on Earth's dusty, red neighbor —were what everyday people hoped for. Even the least informed citizen knew how important the Mars mission was. To have that destroyed? It was unthinkable.

"Where there any survivors?" Amelia asked.

"Some, though we're still waiting for the final reports. What we know right now shows Earth is in a vulnerable position, and we must use every available means to protect the planet and its citizens."

The General took a deep breath. "Earth is overpopulated, and the Taureans need fighters. The Taureans have agreed to an alliance with us. They will provide us with the training and technology to defeat the Xakul, and we will provide them with personnel."

Amelia looked at Oren for confirmation, who simply nodded and said, "We need more warriors. Our numbers are fewer and fewer each year as we battle in the war against the Xakul. What the general says is true."

The general shot a calculating glance between Oren and Amelia and, seeming to come to a snap decision, asked, "We also need medical professionals who can work with both races."

How had everything changed in the space of two days? Amelia looked at the general in disbelief.

With only weeks left on her Space Force contract, and despite her medical experience, she had resigned herself to putting aside her dream of getting off Earth. All she had ever wanted to do was get into space and help people. Could this be her chance? Could he be offering her what she had always wanted?

"Are you offering me a position on a joint mission with the Taureans, sir?"

He smiled, "Yes, I am."

Her eyebrows shot up at his words, and Amelia couldn't

have stopped the broad smile that spread across her face if she had tried.

"Then yes, sir. I am very much up to the task." She looked over at Oren, and the look they shared spoke volumes. This was not the end, it was just the beginning. But the beginning of what, exactly?

CHAPTER THIRTEEN

Oren

Oren watched as the Space Force General nodded at Amelia, then turned to walk towards the Taurean spaceship, accompanied by Domik, leaving him alone with Amelia. The events of the past few days suddenly caught up with him. Now that his team had come for him, and the immediate danger was over, fatigue washed over him like a wave. He leaned back against the Jeep, Amelia settling next to him, her arms crossed. They both watched, transfixed, as human troops swarmed the area, setting up barricades on the road and establishing a defensive perimeter. The place was a mix of activity and noise.

He chuckled to himself and shifted, groaning as the sudden movement made his ribs hurt. "Shit," he said, holding a hand to his side and breathing deeply. The last half hour, being hunted down by that bastard Xakul, had done him no favors.

Amelia shot him a worried look. "Are you going to make

it? You really should get yourself looked at by your own people." She knew she was stating the obvious, but she couldn't bring herself to say what was really on her mind.

Oren gestured towards the bottom of the Taurean ship's ramp, where a group of Taureans and humans were engaging in an animated discussion. It looked as though they were arguing. "And get through that?"

Amelia's answer was lost in the noise of more helicopters as they flew overhead towards the military base. Her brows drew together as she watched them, and she shouted in his ear, "I need to get back to the hospital. There will be people there who need my help."

Then she laughed and was able to speak in a normal tone as the choppers left the area, "You know, Oren, I joined Space Force to get *into* space, which I quickly discovered would never happen." She paused, kicking her boot in the dirt. "I only had a few weeks left on my contract, and I was planning to leave—to go back to being a civilian doctor. I'd had enough, you know? The politics, the red tape... it all felt like a colossal waste of time. But now?" She shook her head and laughed again, but it sounded forced this time. "It's funny how things work out, isn't it?"

"Funny?" Oren wasn't sure what was humorous about the situation.

"Ah, I mean strange. Ironic."

Oren nodded. "Serendipitous?"

"Exactly!"

They shared a smile.

"Amelia, I have a feeling this won't be the last time I see you."

"Oh?"

"If you want, I could have you assigned to the ship I'm on, Starship Zataras?" Oren held his breath in anticipation, trying not to appear as desperate to hear her answer as he was.

"Really? You would do that for me?" She smiled a brilliant smile that lit up her face. "Honestly, even if it's what I've always wanted, it's terrifying to think I'll be in *space* on an *alien* spaceship. It would be awesome to have a familiar face. Even if I've only known you a day." She looked down at her feet, adding quietly, "Although, it feels like I've known you a lot longer than that."

Oren nodded. "Amelia, I owe you a debt of gratitude for helping me the way you have. It's the least I can do."

She looked at him, "Well, um, all I can say is thank you. That would be brilliant."

"Amelia—"

The booming voice of Domik broke into the small bubble that Oren and Amelia had created for themselves, and they sprang back from each other. "Right! Oren! We really have to go before these humans make more demands that I don't have the authority to deal with."

"I should get back to the hospital... yeah." Amelia coughed and eased away from the Jeep to open the driver's door and hoist herself up into the seat.

Oren turned to glare at his brother, who was smirking at him.

"We have to go," Domik repeated. "And you need to get to medical."

Oren reluctantly pulled away from the Jeep and turned to his brother. "Give me a minute, Dom?"

At his brother's nod, Oren leaned into the open driver's

side door, only inches away from Amelia's face. He breathed in deeply, smelling the scent of her shampoo as a slight breeze stirred the cool night air.

"I have a confession," he admitted.

Amelia's lips twitched in amusement. "Oh, and what is that?"

"I'm a selfish bastard."

"Oh... kaay? Amelia laughed, trying not to laugh at his seriousness.

Oren reached towards her, and slid his hand around the back of Amelia's neck. He tugged gently, and she let herself be moved towards him. Eyes meeting, he felt his heart thud in his chest as he gently touched his forehead to hers. "I want you to join us on Zataras, and I'll do everything I can to make that happen. I've *just* met you, and I don't want this to be the last time I see you."

Amelia's eyes crinkled at the sides as she smiled, gently pulling away from his grasp. He took a step back, shutting the Jeep's door. She hit the button for the ignition, the Jeep's engine roaring to life. "I feel the same way, Oren, so you'll get no complaints from me," she said. Throwing the Jeep into gear, she gave him a wink and sped away.

Oren watched as she beeped the horn and waved out the window.

Domik stepped up next to him and looped an arm around Oren's shoulders, helping him towards the shuttle, and up the ramp and inside. He let Domik help him into the small medical bay where he eased himself onto the bed and under the medical scanner.

"You are pretty banged up," his brother said as he hit

the start button on the full body scanner, watching the display.

Warmth spread through Oren's body as the scanner went to work, diagnosing and healing minor injuries and clearing up the bruising on his chest. Giving into the fatigue that had plagued him for the last few days, he relaxed and closed his eyes, one thought in his mind.

He would see her again.

EPILOGUE

Amelia

One month later...

O Today was the day Amelia would finally leave Earth. She walked towards the doors of the hastily built space port, swiping her identity pass against the scanner pad to open them. A computerized voice poured from the speaker, the words also scrolling across the scanner pad.

"Good afternoon, Dr. Amelia O'Malley. Please proceed to waiting lounge two."

Amelia picked up her duffle, grunting as she shouldered the heavy bag, and headed into the building, following the signs to the waiting lounge.

For the past few weeks, Amelia had had hardly any time to herself. She had been interviewed so many times by various Space Force officers that she had become sick of the sound of her own voice. Finally, she had snapped and refused to answer any more questions. They knew more about her than she did herself. After that, she spent much of her time in training.

Amelia was no stranger to cramming for exams, but trying to learn years of Taurean physiology in the space of a few weeks? It was beyond anything she had ever done. She was utterly exhausted. So many hoops to jump through. She had thought that Space Force bureaucracy was bad, but they had nothing on the Taureans. Yesterday had been her final exam, the last test to determine if she knew enough to transfer to a Taurean starship to begin training on their more advanced medical technology.

She had been so focused on her studies that she hadn't allowed herself to think about Oren. But, now that she was joining Starship Zataras? She pressed a hand to her stomach as if it would help with the nervous butterflies she felt. Starship Zataras was essentially a small city, with thousands of crew and support staff. Maybe the chances of them actually running into each other were slim.

But she could hope.

———

The trip to Taurean space had taken two days on a very cramped freighter, which was heading to the same space station where Zataras was due to dock in a few days. Amelia wasn't the only human traveling to join Zataras, but there weren't enough of them to warrant a larger, faster mode of transport. Nor a more comfortable one. So sitting bolt upright in a seat strapped into the freezing cargo hold of a freighter had been Amelia's lot for the last 48 hours. She had finally dropped into a dreamless sleep sometime after hour 34, but her neck had been at an odd angle and now she felt all tight and sore. She was not in a good mood, that's for sure.

So when she walked out of the arrivals processing area and into the space station proper all she wanted was a shower, something to eat, and somewhere to sleep. And in that order.

"Amelia?"

The deep voice slid across her skin like silk and Amelia's head snapped up, looking for the source.

"Oren?"

To be continued...

───────

I promise that Oren and Amelia *will* have their own happy ending! The next instalment of their story is set after the events in Alien Desire, where both Oren and Amelia cameo.

Don't want to miss out? Make sure you're subscribed to my newsletter.

www.melodybeckett.com/newsletter

Read on for more about the next book in the series, Alien Desire...

ALIEN DESIRE

WHAT IF HUMANITY'S ONLY HOPE ISN'T HUMAN?

Space Force veteran Laila Storey thinks she's seen it all—until first contact with an insectoid alien race, the Xakul, destroys a fledgling Martian colony. The Xakul's next target? Earth.

Humanity's only hope is the Taureans, a warrior race who has battled the Xakul and won. Laila must do whatever it takes to save her people, but one particular Taurean warrior proves to be an unwanted distraction.

Commander Zac Qu'Rell wants back in the fight, but his last battle with the Xakul left him badly scarred. The only time he feels at peace is when he's with Laila.

As Zac and Laila work together, temperatures rise, both on and off the battlefield. But there's no time for love.... is there?

———

Read now!

Alien Desire

www.melodybeckett.com/taurean-warriors

ALSO BY MELODY BECKETT

Alien Desire

Alien Seduction

Alien Domination

ABOUT THE AUTHOR

Melody has been a voracious reader of anything with a happy ending since she was old enough to pick up a book. As a teenager she pulled all-nighters reading romance novels under the covers with a torch. She still reads like a fiend, and can always be found with her e-reader within reach!

As a writer, she pens the stories her teenage self wished existed: stories that marry her love for science fiction, action movies, and romance, and stories with happy ever afters.

She hopes you enjoy reading them as much as she enjoys writing them for you!

To keep up to date with Melody's writing and for special offers, sign up to her newsletter on her website.

www.melodybeckett.com/newsletter

a amazon.com/Melody-Beckett/e/B0979QS4MN
BB bookbub.com/profile/melody-beckett

ACKNOWLEDGMENTS

Thanks are due to the Awesome Aspirers, you are all fabulous and your support is so, so very valued. Mwah!

Without the proof reading genius that is Mr B (yes, my husband reads all of my books... even the ones with the sexy bits) there would have been errant apostrophes and wayward commas. Thank you for all your support... and every cup of coffee you've silently delivered when I'm deep in thought. You're one in a million, my love.

And lastly, but definitely not least, thank you to my readers. Your lovely emails and reviews are always so very welcome, and encouraging.

Happy reading!

Mel x